W9-DDK-596

# United in Freedom

Marcia Lynch

Cover Illustration: Paul Micich
Inside Illustration: Sue Cornelison

**About the Author**

Marcia Lynch was born in Chicago, Illinois, where she lived until she moved to California with her husband, Jay. They raised two sons there.

As a middle school teacher, Ms. Lynch integrated the subjects she taught, English and history. She selected historical novels for her students to read to enhance their learning as they studied a specific period in American history. Because she saw a need for a Civil War novel, Ms. Lynch wrote *Twins. United in Freedom* is a sequel to her first novel.

Ms. Lynch enjoys her grandchildren, writing, reading, and boating. She and her husband live in Huntington Beach, California.

**Dedication**

To all of you who encouraged me, especially Wilma.

Text © 2000 by Perfection Learning® Corporation.
All rights reserved. No part of this book may be used or reproduced in any manner whatsoever without written permission from the publisher.
Printed in the United States of America. For information, contact
Perfection Learning® Corporation
1000 North Second Avenue, P.O. Box 500
Logan, Iowa 51546-0500
Phone: 1-800-831-4190
Fax: 1-712-644-2392

Paperback ISBN 0-7891-5102-2
Cover Craft® ISBN 0-7807-9068-5
Printed in the U.S.A.

**6 7 8 9 10 PP 08 07 06 05 04 03**

# CONTENTS

# Chapter 1
# THOMAS'S CHANCE

Now's my chance, Thomas thought. He tiptoed down the back steps.

The master's family was at a Fourth of July party. And all the slaves had the day off.

Six-year-old Thomas hurried out the back door of the Big House. He ran to the cookhouse. There he searched for food to take with him.

Thomas spied some corn bread on the table. He grabbed as much as he could hold. But that wasn't very much. So he found a napkin and wrapped it around more bread.

After searching some more, Thomas found some ham. He unwrapped the napkin and put the ham inside too.

It sure smells good! Thomas thought. He put a small piece in his mouth. He closed his eyes and enjoyed the seldom-tasted meat.

Then Thomas ran back to the Big House. He quickly climbed the stairs. He was careful that no one saw him.

Thomas remembered there was a traveling bag in Master Paul's chest. He quickly found it.

Looking through Paul's clothes, Thomas found a shirt and a pair of pants. He stuffed them into the bag. Then he put the food inside. Now he was ready!

Thomas planned to escape just as his dad and his twin brother, Henry, had. They were the only family he had, and he would find them.

It was late afternoon and sunny. But clouds had begun to form in the west. Thomas looked at them, but he gave them no thought.

Thomas knew where north was by the position of the sun. So he began to walk across the huge fields.

Thomas walked as fast as he could. His only

thought was that he would find his father and brother. But he had little idea of where they might be.

Thomas had looked in Paul's geography book. When the tutor was showing Paul the northern states, Thomas had tried to listen. He remembered Pennsylvania. And he knew that was where he was going.

By the time Thomas had walked a while, he was tired. He was also hot, dirty, and hungry.

Great dark clouds began rolling across the sky. The sun began to go down. Thomas was a little afraid. But he bravely tried to remember why he was running away. And this helped for a little while.

As soon as the sun set, the thunder began. Huge raindrops hit Thomas. He knew he had to find cover. But where? Where could he find a place out of the rain?

Thomas was soaking wet. The ground beneath his feet was muddy and slippery. He could hardly see ahead of the pouring rain. And it was dark. Thomas began to get scared.

Then Thomas saw a large dark shape ahead. A tree! He ran to it and stepped under its branches. The thick, heavy leaves of the tree protected him from the rain.

Gratefully, Thomas sat down. He leaned against the huge tree trunk and dug in his bag for food. He was really hungry. Without thinking of tomorrow, he ate all the food.

The thunder and lightning continued, and Thomas was still scared. He took Master Paul's shirt and pants out of the bag. Then he lay on the ground and covered himself with the clothes.

---

"Wake up!" someone was yelling. "Wake up, you little thief!"

Thomas was being roughly shaken. He opened his eyes and looked into William's mean face.

"What are you doing, boy?" William yelled as he shook Thomas. "Were you trying to run away? How far did you think you could go?"

Thomas began to cry. He couldn't have answered any of William's questions even if he wanted to.

As overseer on the plantation, William often treated the slaves harshly. William roughly jerked Thomas to his feet. He stuffed the clothes into the bag and slung Thomas onto a horse. Then William got on. He jerked on the horse's reins, and it galloped back to the plantation.

William rode around to the back of the Big House. He stopped in front of a little-used shed that was almost covered with brush. He jumped down and then jerked Thomas down off the horse.

William thrust Thomas inside the shed. Then he

slammed the door. Thomas could hear something heavy being dragged in front of the door.

Thomas knew he was in trouble. Would he be beaten as Ezekial had been? How long would he have to stay in this horrible place?

Thomas tried to control his crying. Then he felt something small and furry run over his legs. A rat was in the shed!

"Get off me!" Thomas cried as he jumped up. "Get off me!" Thomas jumped up and began banging on the door. But no one heard him.

Afraid to sit down because of the rat, Thomas stood by the door. He hoped that someone would rescue him soon.

After a long time, the shed door opened. William grabbed Thomas and dragged him out.

"Now you're in for it," laughed William. "We're going to see Master Walker."

Thomas began crying again. He tried to get his arm free from William's firm grasp.

Then Thomas saw something that took his breath away. He was being taken to the whipping post!

William tied Thomas's arms around the post. Then Master Walker came and stood in front of Thomas.

"Thomas," Master Walker said. "What happened to

Ezekial when he tried to run away?"

Thomas was so afraid that he couldn't answer.

Master Walker took Thomas's chin in his large hand. He tipped Thomas's face up and looked directly into his eyes. "You tell me, Thomas," Master Walker demanded. "Right now!"

"He g-g-g-got a wh-wh-whipping," Thomas managed to get out between sobs.

"You're only six years old," said Master Walker. "And I'm not going to whip you this time. But you must never try to run away again.

"I've let you be with my son, Paul," Master Walker continued. "But you could be working in the tobacco fields."

Thomas nodded his head. The tears still streamed down his cheeks.

"Now, Thomas, give me your promise," ordered Master Walker.

"I won't ever run away again," Thomas sobbed. "I promise."

"Untie him," Master Walker ordered William.

"But, Master Walker," said William. "He's got to be punished."

"I make the decisions around here!" said Master Walker. "Now untie him!"

William untied Thomas. But he did it slowly.

"I'm not going to whip a six-year-old boy,"

continued Master Walker. "Now go wash your face, Thomas. And take your place with Master Paul. He needs you."

"Yes, sir," Thomas said as he ran off.

Chapter 2

# THE REST OF THE STORY

"I want to show you how I clean the barn, Dad," Henry said proudly. He led Byron into the barn. "Uncle Josiah showed me how to clean the horse stalls. I keep the place where we milk the cows clean too."

Byron's heart swelled with pride when he saw what a good job Henry was doing. His mama would be proud, Byron thought.

Josiah walked in just then. “I never have to tell Henry to do his chores,” he said. “He takes pride in his work. He sure takes after you, Byron.”

“Thank you, Josiah,” said Byron. “I’m proud of Henry too.”

Byron and Josiah watched Henry until he was done. Then they went to the house for lunch.

Sally was just putting fried pork chops and potatoes on the table. The smell of freshly baked bread filled the room. Henry could hardly wait to finish the prayer and begin eating.

The creamy butter melted into the delicious white bread. Henry loved every mouthful.

Later, everyone finished their blueberry cobbler and settled back.

“Let’s hear the rest of your story, Byron,” Josiah said.

Byron thought for a moment. A few days ago, he had begun to tell the Turners and Henry about his life as a slave. How he and his mother had been taken from their home in Africa. How they were taken across the ocean and then sold into slavery.

“My mother and I got used to our new lives quickly,” Byron continued.

***I learned the new language. But it was harder for my mother.***

*We worked every day in the tobacco fields. Then we ate in front of the cookhouse and slept in shacks. We did the same thing every day but Sunday.*

*After a few weeks, my mother got very sick. She had chills. And she threw up a lot.*

*Martha came to help my mother. She knew right away that Mother had malaria. She knew about medicine and how to read.*

*Before Martha came to Rolling Acres, she had lived with a woman who was a midwife. As the old woman's eyesight failed, she had depended more and more on Martha. Many cures and tonics were written in the old woman's books. The old woman had taught Martha to read, which was against the law.*

*The old woman had died when Martha was 15. Then Martha had been bought by Master Walker.*

*I went to stay with Martha until my mother could get better. But she was too sick. She never got better.*

*Everyone tried to comfort me after my mother died. But I cried and cried. She was my only family.*

*William, the overseer, came to the burial. He told me I was to live with Martha.*

*I felt so alone. But as I grew, Martha became like a mother to me.*

*When I was about ten, Master Walker planned a big party. It was to last for three or four days. And all the guests would stay on the plantation.*

***All the slaves had to help get ready for the party. The plantation carpenter showed me how to hold a hammer. He taught me how to make a table. I thought it was fun.***

***My tables had straight legs and were level. Soon I started working with the carpenter instead of working in the fields. He showed me all he knew about woodworking. And I liked it.***

***Elizabeth and I got married when we were about 18. And soon after, she told me that we were going to have a baby.***

***I was so happy! I ran all over telling everyone the good news.***

***But during the birthing, Elizabeth began bleeding heavily. And after the twins were born, she died.***

"Twins!" interrupted Henry. "Who were the twins? Were they born before me?"

"Hush, Henry," Byron said. "And let me tell you. Yes—two baby boys. And your mother named you Henry and your brother, Thomas."

Then Byron told the rest of the story. About how he'd run away from the plantation with Henry. And how he'd had to leave a sickly Thomas behind.

"I promised I'd return to get Thomas," Byron said. "And I will!"

"There's one more thing," Byron continued. "Look at your hands, Henry. See how your little fingers are crooked? Well, Thomas's little fingers are crooked too."

Henry stared at his fingers. "I've got a brother, Dad? When can we go get him? Let's go right now!" He stood up.

"Sit down, son," Byron said. "As soon as we can, we'll go."

"We'd be happy to have your other son here with us," said Sally with tears in her eyes.

"You've had a hard life, Byron," Josiah said. "I hope these last few years have been easier for you."

Josiah and Sally had taken Byron and baby Henry in years ago when they had first escaped to Harrisburg. For the last six years, the Turners had done everything they could to help Henry and his dad.

Byron was now known as a skilled woodworker. He and Henry had their own small home near the Turners' house.

"You know how happy I am here," said Byron. "And I'm happy that Henry will never have to go through what I did. That's why I've got to get Thomas soon."

Then, without warning, chills swept over Byron. He could no longer sit up. He slumped to the floor as Josiah and Sally rushed forward to help.

"H-H-Henry," Byron chattered.

"Dad! Dad!" Henry cried as he leaned over Byron.

Byron, still shaking, tried to sit up with Josiah's help. "M-m-malaria attack," he said weakly. "Get me home. Won't be any trouble."

"Henry can sleep in our house," said Josiah. "Then Byron can be in his own bed."

"Henry, go get some clothes," said Sally. "We'll help your dad get to his bed. And you can sleep in the spare room."

Sally and Josiah managed to get a shaking Byron to his cabin. Josiah helped Byron into bed and covered him.

"Henry," said Sally. "Bring some quilts from the house over here for your dad. He's mighty cold."

"Let's let him sleep now," Josiah said. "I'll check on him later."

At the Turners' house, Henry dried the dishes while Sally washed. "How would you like to go to school, Henry?" asked Sally. "Now that you're six, you're old enough to learn to read. Would you like that?"

"I sure would, Miss Sally," said Henry.

Sally was the teacher at the Quaker school down the road. Henry had never been there. But he knew that many children went there.

"I'll teach you so you can read to yourself," said Sally. "And you can read to us too."

"I'd really like that, Miss Sally," said Henry. "And I know my dad would like it too. When can I go?"

"School doesn't start until after the crops are in," said Sally. "So you can start in about six weeks. And we can walk there together every day."

"I'm going over to Christiana for a few days," Byron said to Henry. "I'll be helping build a barn for Mr. Stevens. And I think you're old enough to go with me.

"We can take our quilts and sleep by the fire," Byron continued. "You can learn about building."

"I'd like to go, Dad!" said Henry excitedly. "And I can help too! I know I can! I'm going to tell Miss Sally that I'm going with you!"

Later, Mr. Stevens pulled into the yard with his wagon. Byron spoke to Mr. Stevens while pointing to Henry. Mr. Stevens grinned in agreement.

"Come on, Henry," Byron called. "Get your stuff! And let's go!"

For the next few hours, Henry played in the back of the wagon.

As Byron, Henry, and Mr. Stevens neared town, they heard loud shouting and gunshots. Ahead, they could see clouds of dust swirling through the air.

"I wonder what's going on," Mr. Stevens said. He

pulled the wagon to the roadside and began to climb down.

As Mr. Stevens stepped to the ground, he saw three men on horseback. They were riding toward the wagon. Mr. Stevens took off his hat and waved it in the air. He was signaling the men to stop.

"What's happening up there?" Mr. Stevens asked the men. "Who's shooting? And why?"

The three riders stopped.

"There's a riot going on," said one rider. "Some folks are protesting the old Fugitive Slave Law."

"Yeah," another rider added. "The law that says we've got to return all escaped slaves to their owners."

"There are folks from both sides of the issue going at it in town," the first rider said.

"I'd better turn around and go a different way home," said Mr. Stevens. "I don't want to put Byron and Henry in danger."

"You're smart to do that," the riders agreed. Then they mounted their horses and rode away.

"I'm sure we won't get into trouble going this way, Byron," Mr. Stevens said as he climbed into the wagon.

# Chapter 3
# ROYAL

Ten-year-old Thomas was in Paul's room polishing his master's boots. He looked up as Paul rushed into the room.

"Look, Thomas," Paul said. "I found this book." Paul held out the copy of *Uncle Tom's Cabin* and Thomas read the title aloud.

"We can read it," Paul continued. "I think it's about slavery." He sat down on the floor and showed Thomas the first page.

"Where did you get it?" asked Thomas. "If Master Walker finds me reading, I'll get a whipping, for sure."

"It was in my dad's trash," said Paul. "So I took it. He won't miss it. I'll hide it under my mattress. We'll read it whenever we get the chance.

"Dad is talking a lot about people hating slavery," Paul continued. "Maybe we can learn more about it from this book."

Later in the day, Paul carefully took the book out from under his mattress. Then he sat down next to Thomas.

As Paul opened the book, a sheet of paper fell out. It was a letter. Paul read it aloud.

DEAR MR. WALKER,

READ THIS BOOK IF YOU DARE. KNOW THAT MANY OF US SOUTHERNERS HATE SLAVERY. YOU SHOULD PAY YOUR SLAVES OR FREE THEM.

A FRIEND

"Let's start reading, Thomas!" said Paul.

"That's a fine-looking horse, Byron!" said Josiah. Henry and Byron proudly rode toward the barn. "You've needed one for a long time."

Byron and Henry got off the horse. Josiah walked all around the rust-colored horse.

"He looks healthy," said Josiah.

Byron grinned and patted the horse's head.

"Sally and I were talking just a bit ago," said Josiah. "You've done a lot in the ten years you've been here."

Sally joined the group. "Here, Henry," she said. "I'm sure the horse will like this." She handed Henry an apple. "What are you going to name him? Or does he already have a name?"

"Hmm," Byron said. "We'll have to think of a good name, won't we, Henry? No one said anything about a name when I bought him."

The horse was a beautiful animal. With a bit of cleaning, his rust-colored coat would be shiny. With a little brushing, his mane and tail would be thick and fluffy.

He was an old horse, though. And his back was a little swayed. But he would be fine for Henry and Byron.

The horse was enjoying the apple. He gently bit into it as Henry held it.

"We should name him Royal," Henry said. "I just finished reading about a dog named Royal. Remember, Miss Sally? The dog in that story?"

"Yes, that was a good story," Sally smiled.

"Okay," said Byron. "We'll name him Royal. I'm going to pay for his keep in the stable. And for the food he eats. I'm going to get him real healthy. Then we can think about making that trip back to Virginia for Thomas."

Byron remembered the message he'd gotten years ago from Martha. She had written the note warning him not to return to the plantation for Thomas. Slave hunters were everywhere. Byron had been heartbroken.

In his heart, he had known the time was not right. And he also knew that Thomas would be well cared for.

"Now that Henry can write so well," Byron continued, "we're going to send Thomas a message. We'll tell him that I'm coming soon. Garrett can take it to the plantation."

Ten years before, Garrett had helped Byron and Henry escape. Garrett had led them from Virginia to Sally and Josiah's home near Harrisburg. Frequently, Garrett would stop by to visit on his many trips helping others.

Henry's face lit up. "Can I go to Virginia with you, Dad?" he asked. His voice became higher as he spoke. "We can both ride on Royal, can't we? I can hardly wait to see my brother! When are we going? Let's go tomorrow!" He was so excited that he was jumping up and down.

Byron put his arm out to stop Henry's wild jumping. "Now calm down, Henry," he said. "I don't know when I'll be able to go. We have to wait for the right time."

"Can I go? Can I go?" Henry kept asking. He realized that his father had not answered that question.

But before Byron could reply, Josiah said, "Bring Royal this way, Byron. We'll put him in the second stall. It has clean hay in it. And you can use some of my brushes. He could do with a good cleaning."

Byron and Josiah showed Henry how to care for the horse. And how to feed him. Henry had to stand on a stool to get the feed bag over Royal's head. But he didn't seem to mind.

---

After supper that night, Byron and Henry returned to their cabin. They began to talk about the message they would send to Thomas.

"We'll send the message to Martha," said Byron.

"She's the only one who knows how to read. Now what should our message say?"

"Let's just say 'Dear Thomas, we are coming to get you. Love, Dad and Henry,' " said Henry. "I'll get some paper from school tomorrow. And then I can write the message tomorrow night."

"Henry," Byron said. "Please listen to me. It's not going to be possible for you to make the trip with me. We can't fit three people on one horse. You'll have to stay here. You can keep going to school and learning."

Henry's face fell. He knew that his dad was right. But how could he be patient and wait? It was going to be very hard.

"Okay, Dad," Henry agreed. "I guess you're right. I don't want my brother to have to walk. Because I know it's a long way." He sighed.

Byron smiled proudly at his son. He wished Elizabeth could see what a fine boy her son had grown to be.

"So how about my reading lesson?" Byron asked.

Henry smiled and ran to get the book he had brought home from school.

A few weeks later, Garrett stopped by to see how Byron and Henry were. Josiah and Sally always welcomed him. They were always interested and wanted to help him in any way they could.

After Sally's delicious supper, Byron asked Garrett about delivering the message. Henry proudly gave Garrett the note.

"I'll find a way to get this message to Martha," Garrett said. "It won't be easy. But I'm going to do it. I know how important it is. And we want Thomas to be ready."

Garrett carefully placed the note in his bag's special pouch. "I'm going to be leaving in the morning," he said. "There's a family of four waiting to come north. I'll stop here again, Byron. And maybe we can travel together when you go to get Thomas."

# Chapter 4
## Getting the Message

Master Walker snatched the book from Thomas's hands. "Where did you learn to read?" he shouted angrily. "Slaves aren't supposed to read!"

Thomas's heart was pounding. He wanted to say something. But he knew he wasn't allowed to. He knew he must be brave. But he was afraid. He remembered when he'd almost gotten a whipping once before.

"I can't have you reading!" Master Walker shouted. He began shaking Thomas as tears fell down Thomas's cheeks. "You know it's wrong!"

Hearing his dad's shouts, Paul ran quickly up the stairs. He had just returned from riding.

"Dad!" Paul cried. "What's wrong?"

Then Paul realized what had happened. He saw his book on the floor.

Talking in a calm voice, Paul got his father to sit down on a chair. Even at ten, he knew how to work around his father's outbursts. He wondered why his father was so angry all of the time.

Paul sat down beside his father. He tried to explain about Thomas and his reading.

"When I have my lessons, Thomas is always here," Paul said. "Don't you always tell him to be near me in case I need something?

"Well, as I learned to read, Thomas did too," Paul confessed. "He could even answer the questions. Sometimes, we talk about what we read."

Master Walker's eyebrows shot up.

"Thomas has been reading for four years now," Paul continued.

Master Walker took a deep breath. "Paul, you're not too young to know what people are saying," he said. "They're speaking out against slavery. They say we shouldn't own people. That we should let them earn money for their work.

"But those people don't realize how well we take care of our slaves," Master Walker continued. "And if somebody like Thomas runs away, it hurts the plantation. Now, what else has he learned?"

Instead of speaking to Thomas, Master Walker continued to talk to Paul. It was as if Thomas were not in the room.

"That's all, Dad," Paul said. "We just talk about the reading. It helps me understand the stories better."

Paul was sure that Thomas could do sums too. He thought he probably knew geography. But Paul didn't want to anger his father any more. So he kept quiet.

"From now on, Thomas will not be in the room during lessons," demanded Master Walker. "Is that understood? Is that clear? Stand up and promise, Paul."

Reluctantly, Paul stood up. He moved closer to where his father sat. "I promise, Father. Thomas will leave the room during lessons," he said. But he crossed his fingers behind his back.

Paul knew that Thomas was smart. Maybe even smarter than he was. And it helped when he and Thomas talked about the readings.

Paul wouldn't let Thomas leave during lessons. He'd just be careful not to let his father find out.

---

As dusk fell, Garrett came out of his safe place. He began to sneak around Richmond, keeping to the shadows.

Byron's message was in Garrett's bag. And he was determined to find a way to get it to the Walker plantation.

Just then, Garrett heard shouting. As he drew closer, he could see a large wagon being loaded by black men.

"Hurry up! Hurry up!" one of the men shouted. "I should've been on my way by now! You are too slow!"

Garrett thought he knew the voice. As he got nearer, he could see it was William, the overseer from the Walker plantation.

Garrett was glad to see the wagon. The slaves could help him get the message to Martha. But it would be hard to hide the note.

Garrett continued watching. Soon it was dark. He noticed that the moon was not out.

Then Garrett saw William walk into the store. He left the wagon unattended.

Now's my chance, Garrett thought. He crept to the wagon. No one seemed to be around. Garrett saw bags of flour, bolts of cloth, plants, and seed boxes on the wagon.

Garrett remembered that Martha usually took care of the flower garden. He quickly opened a seed box. He put Byron's folded note inside. Martha should find it. Her name was written on the outside. Then Garrett quickly closed the box and shoved it under the others.

At that moment, Garrett heard William. "I'm all set now," William said. "And I'm going to be on my way. See you next time I come to town."

Garrett quickly ran into the shadows. But he continued to watch as William drove away. He sighed with relief as the wagon headed down the road.

By sundown of the next day, William had stopped by Martha's cabin. "I brought seeds and plants from town," he shouted. "And Mistress Walker wants them planted in the morning. Be out front at dawn!"

Martha came to the door of her cabin. "Yes, William," she replied. "I'll be there."

Martha walked to the front of the Big House the next morning. The sun was just rising into a beautiful blue, cloudless sky. Planting always made her happy. And her heart lifted as she saw the beautiful plants on the back of the wagon.

Mistress Walker appeared. She greeted Martha. "Looks like it's going to be a beautiful day. A great day for planting," she said pleasantly.

"Is there anything special that you want me to do?" asked Martha. She began taking the plants out of the wagon.

"You always do a nice job," said Mistress Walker. "I'll leave it up to you. I'll stop back out later this afternoon." Mistress Walker headed into the house.

Martha nodded her head in reply. Then she began walking down the path with the flowers. Some were already blooming. She began setting new plants down where she thought they should go.

Martha returned to the wagon for the seed boxes. She saw that one box was unsealed. Inside, she saw a folded piece of paper with her name on it.

Without opening the note, Martha put it inside the bodice of her dress. She dared not read it now. Watching eyes were everywhere.

Just as the sun was setting, Mistress Walker returned for the second time. "My, Martha!" she exclaimed. "You've done a wonderful job! And so quickly too.

"I'll have William clean up the empty pots," Mistress Walker said. "And he can put away the shovels and hoes. You go on and have your supper."

"Thank you, ma'am," Martha said. Then she hurried off. All day long, she had thought about the paper. What could it be? she wondered.

After supper, Martha cautiously took out the paper. As she read it, a big grin spread across her face.

Martha quietly motioned to Nancy. As they walked

away from the others, Martha told her that Byron was alive. And he was coming for Thomas.

Nancy was excited too. "How are you going to get the message to Thomas?" she asked.

"I'm going to have to wait until Sunday," Martha said. "That's when he usually comes over here. It's going to be hard to wait for four days. Now don't tell anyone else. It's our secret."

# Chapter 5
# Tragedy

"Be careful," said Josiah Turner. Byron leaned down from the horse and they grasped hands. "We'll pray for you to have a safe journey."

"Thank you," Byron answered. He leaned down one more time to touch Henry's shoulder. "I'll be back as soon as I can. And Thomas will be with me!"

"Don't you worry about Henry," Sally assured him.

"He'll be safe with us."

The Turners and Henry watched as Byron rode away. No one knew what dangers lay ahead for Byron.

Sally put her arm around Henry as they walked back to the house. "I'll get supper ready. You can help me, Henry."

Early the next morning, Sally, Josiah, and Henry were awakened by the sound of horses. Henry peeked out his window.

Two men on horseback rode into the Turners' yard. One of them was leading his dad's horse. And Byron was lying across the horse's back!

The Turners and Henry dashed outside at the same time. "What happened? Where? How?" they asked all at once.

The two men got off their horses. "We thought you might know this man," said the shorter man. "We came across the horse last night. Not very far from here. We knew that there must be a rider for the horse. But we couldn't see anything. So we camped there by the horse and waited for daylight."

"We found the body not very far away," said the other man. "He must have hit a low branch that knocked him off the horse. The horse led us here this morning."

"No!" Sally cried out. Then she put her arm around Henry and led him to the side of the yard. They stood there together while Josiah and the two men lifted Henry's body off the horse.

"How old is the boy?" asked the short man.

"He just turned eleven," Josiah answered sadly. "Byron here was on his way to rescue his other son. He's still on the plantation in Virginia where Byron used to work."

"We're both real sorry," the short man said. "We'd be glad to help you move his body into the house."

The three men carried Byron's body into the house.

Henry followed slowly. Great sobs racked his body.

"Hush, hush, now," Sally said as she tried to calm him. "We're your parents now, Henry. Me and Josiah."

The two men followed Josiah as he went to get a shovel. Then they helped him dig a grave in the woods beyond the farm.

After the men had dug the grave, they wrapped Byron's body in his bed quilt. It was the one with the blue and white star-burst pattern. Then they carried Byron's body to the grave site.

Josiah told briefly of Byron's life, hopes, and dreams. And then Byron was gently buried with God's blessing.

# Chapter 6

## 1857

"Look, Thomas!" cried Paul as he rushed into his bedroom. "I just found this!" He was waving a newspaper. "My dad had this on his desk."

Thomas, nearly 14 years old now, was cleaning Paul's rifle. He set it down and walked over to where Paul was now sitting.

" 'Dred Scott Must Remain a Slave,' " Paul read.

Then Paul read the newspaper article aloud. Thomas followed along over Paul's shoulder.

The two boys learned that Dred Scott was a slave. His master had taken him to a free state. Then the master died. Dred Scott believed he should now be free. So he sued in a court of law to keep his freedom.

Chief Justice Tanney ruled against Dred Scott. He said that a Negro had no rights and could not sue in a court of law.

As Paul and Thomas read further, they learned that many Northerners were upset with the decision. Rallies and riots were taking place in many towns. However, Southerners were happy about the ruling. They believed that once someone was a slave, he was always a slave.

"What do you think, Thomas?" Paul asked.

"I don't think it's fair," Thomas answered. "Aren't slaves people too?"

"My dad says he doesn't think he can manage the plantation without slave labor," said Paul. "But I'm beginning to think that slaves should be free. But don't tell anyone I said that."

"I'm glad to hear you say that, Master Paul," said Thomas. "I'm afraid it's going to be a long time before slaves will be free. But one day, it will happen."

Then Thomas changed the subject. "While you

were out, I got your clothes ready for the fox hunt tomorrow morning. And for your dinner party tomorrow night.

"Paul, since you're going to be mighty busy tomorrow, could I spend the day with Martha?" Thomas asked. "I haven't seen her for a long time."

"Oh, sure," Paul said. He turned and looked at the clothes that were laid out. "But be back after the fox hunt so you can help me get dressed for the party. I am anxious to see Susan. It's been two months. And I've missed her."

Thomas ran to Martha's cabin. He quietly knocked on her door.

"Thomas!" Martha cried as she opened her door. "How wonderful to see you!" She locked Thomas in a big hug. "I hope it's okay with Master Paul that you're here."

"It is, Martha," Thomas said. "He's going fox hunting. So I don't have to be back until he returns."

Martha finally let Thomas go. He walked into the cabin as Martha shut the door.

"I wanted to talk with you about my dad and Henry," Thomas said. "In a few weeks, Henry and I are going to be 14 years old. It's been almost four years since we got that note saying my dad was coming for me. Something terrible has happened."

Martha felt the same as Thomas. But she didn't want to make matters worse. "Now, Thomas," she began, trying to reassure him. "I'm sure your dad has good reason for not being here yet. He'll be here as soon as he can.

"I'll try to send a message to Garrett," Martha continued. "We haven't seen him for a long time. But maybe he can tell us what's keeping your dad."

# 7 Chapter

# JOSEPHINE

The night before his eighteenth birthday, Henry packed his bag. He had an extra shirt, a small knife, and a canteen full of water. Aunt Sally would pack some food for him in the morning.

Henry carried his bedroll out to the stables. Then he'd be ready in the morning.

Henry thought about the years since his father's death. He had finished his schooling at age 14. And then he had begun doing carpentry work.

By saving his money, Henry had been able to buy a new, younger horse. And now he felt he was ready to make the trip to Virginia.

Many Southerners still used slaves. And the Northerners were still upset and angry about it.

Preachers, speakers on street corners, and the newspapers talked about the evils of slavery. There was even talk of fighting—going to war. And Henry knew he had to get Thomas before that happened.

As the sun rose, Josiah and Sally said good-bye to Henry.

"Be sure to travel by night when you cross into Virginia," warned Josiah. "The paper I wrote says you are free. But I doubt if any Southerners would believe it.

"And there are still many slave hunters out there," Josiah continued. "So be careful. I sure wish Garrett were here to go with you."

Sally tucked several packets of food in Henry's bag. Then Henry tied the bag and the bedroll behind the saddle.

Henry hugged his two friends. Then he quickly mounted the horse and began his journey.

Henry rode in the near darkness of the early sunrise. He'd been traveling for six nights. And he was certain he was in Virginia—a slave state.

Henry knew he must be extra careful. He kept to the least-traveled paths as much as possible.

Henry knew there was talk of war. The South and the North were preparing to fight. So Henry wanted to find Thomas and return home as quickly as possible.

Henry was lost in thought. He didn't hear the hoofbeats coming in his direction until it was too late. He looked at the ground, hoping to pass the riders without incident.

"Well, what do we have here?" said one of the riders. He stopped right in front of Henry so his horse couldn't move. The white man pulled his rifle from the saddle and lazily aimed it at Henry's stomach.

The man with the gun was young. Probably no more than 20. Another young man stopped alongside of Henry's horse.

"Put up your hands," said the man with the rifle.

So Henry did. He hoped that by doing what the men said, they'd let him go.

The second man jumped down from his horse. He walked over to Henry.

"Get down," the man ordered.

Henry slid off the horse and put up his hands. He didn't know what to do besides stand patiently.

"Samuel, check for weapons," said the man with the rifle.

Samuel's hands patted Henry's clothes. "Nothing here, Charlie," he replied.

Then Samuel walked over to Henry's horse. He found Henry's knife in the bag.

"This is it, Charlie," Samuel said, holding up the knife. "Except for some clothes and food."

"Where are you from, boy?" Charlie asked, still pointing the rifle at Henry. "Are you running away from your master?"

"No," Henry replied, his heart wildly beating. "I'm a free man. And I have the papers to prove it."

"We don't care about your papers," said Samuel.

Samuel took a length of rope from his saddle. He tied Henry's hands behind his back. Then he tied a rope around Henry's neck.

Samuel mounted his horse. He was still holding the other end of the rope that was around Henry's neck.

Samuel prodded his horse. Henry was pulled along behind. The horse wasn't going very fast. But Henry had to run to keep from stumbling.

Charlie followed along behind Henry, keeping the rifle pointed at him. Charlie led Henry's horse too.

After a while, Samuel and Charlie finally stopped.

This must be their home, thought Henry. He was bent over, trying to catch his breath.

Samuel roughly pulled Henry in front of a small wooden shed. It was almost covered over with huge trees and leaves.

"We'll keep you here until we decide what to do with you," said Samuel. "Maybe we can make some money by selling you back to your master."

"But, I'm a free man from Harris—," Henry tried to say. But he couldn't finish. He was roughly shoved inside the shed.

Henry heard the key turn in the padlock. He knew he was locked in. After a moment, he heard hoofbeats moving away from the shed.

Henry's eyes slowly adjusted to the darkness. He could tell that the shed was very small. And from the smell, he knew it had a dirt floor.

Henry's hands were still tied behind him. His arms ached, but he struggled to free his hands. After much work, he was able to get them free. Then he untied the rope from around his neck.

There was nothing to do now but try to get some rest. So Henry sat down and leaned back in a corner of the shed.

When Henry awoke, he could see shafts of light entering the shed. There was a hole in the roof.

Henry was tired, hungry, and thirsty. But there was nothing he could do. He looked around the shed. He couldn't see any way to escape.

The light through the hole in the roof faded. By now, Henry was feeling weak from lack of food and water. But just as dusk arrived, he heard footsteps outside the shed. A key scraped in the padlock. The door opened.

Henry expected to see Samuel and Charlie. But instead, he saw a young slave girl.

The young girl took a few steps into the shed.

Then she set down a small bowl and a canteen. Henry lifted the napkin that covered it. He saw grits and bread. Henry's stomach began to rumble with hunger.

Henry ate and drank. The girl watched without saying a word. Henry couldn't remember when grits and bread had tasted so good!

"My name is Henry," he said. "Thanks for the food and water. Who are you? And where are Samuel and Charlie?"

"Samuel and Charlie have gone off to fight," replied the girl. "Charlie said they wouldn't be gone more than two or three days.

"My name is Josephine," she added. "Charlie told me to feed you once a day.

"They told me if you escaped, they'd kill me when they returned," Josephine said. "And I know they'll do it. They're mean."

Henry listened to Josephine. He saw what a beautiful girl she was. Her brown eyes were shadowed by long, dark lashes. She was not much shorter than he was. Henry could not take his eyes off her.

Josephine told Henry that her parents were both dead. "I have no family left," she said sadly.

Henry explained who he was and why he was in Virginia.

"I know I can't get to Thomas now," Henry finished. "So I'm going back North. You could come with me. You could be free!"

Josephine agreed immediately.

"I'll go back to the cookhouse and get us some food and water," she offered. "What else will we need?"

"Bring a knife if you can find one," Henry replied. "Hurry, now, and get our supplies. We can get a good head start if we leave right away."

# Chapter 8

# THOMAS GOES TO WAR

"Thomas! Thomas!" Paul shouted. His horse skidded to a halt just outside the stable door.

"I'm here, Master Paul," Thomas said. He had run out of the stable when he heard the rapid hoofbeats approaching.

Thomas grabbed the horse's reins as Paul leaped to the ground.

"We're going to war, Thomas!" Paul cried. "I just enlisted in J.E.B. Stuart's First Regiment of Virginia Cavalry.

"I met Captain Stuart," Paul continued breathlessly. "And I knew I wanted to fight in the war with him. And now that I'm 18, I can!"

Paul walked with Thomas into the stable. He kept talking as Thomas removed the saddle from Paul's horse.

Thomas began rubbing and brushing the horse. Paul became more excited as he told Thomas about Captain Stuart.

"He was wearing a plumed hat and scarlet cape," Paul said. "He stood out from all the other men in Richmond.

"And then I heard him speak," Paul continued. "With Captain Stuart in command, I know we'll wipe out those Union soldiers. I signed up to fight right then and there."

Thomas put Paul's horse in its stall. Then he turned to Paul. "What did you mean that we were going?" Thomas asked.

"I need you there, Thomas," Paul said. "To take care of my horse, food, and clothes. Most of my friends are taking their servants too.

"I'm going to tell my father right now," Paul said as he grabbed his saddlebag. "And then we'll get our things together. We're leaving in the morning." He hurried off toward the Big House before Thomas had a chance to say anything.

Thomas was a little afraid of leaving home. But he was also excited about going with Paul. Thomas knew he wouldn't be allowed to fight. And he didn't want to.

Thomas gave the horse some oats. Then he left the stables.

Thomas decided he'd better start packing Paul's things. So he went into the Big House. As he passed Master Walker's office, he heard him speaking.

"I'm proud of you, son," Master Walker told Paul. "I know you'll make the Walker family proud."

"I must leave in the morning, Father," Paul said. "Thomas and I have to get our things ready. I'll tell Mother at supper."

"She won't be happy," said Paul's father. "But she'll understand."

As Paul ran out of the office, he nearly knocked Thomas over.

"Come on, Thomas!" Paul said.

In Paul's room, Thomas began picking through some of Paul's clothing. "We'll need some traveling bags, Master Paul," said Thomas. "Where can I get some?"

Paul opened his saddlebag and pulled out several bags. "They gave me these when I signed up," Paul said. "They also gave me a canteen.

"I'll get my rifle and uniform when I report tomorrow," Paul continued. "So don't take any of my clothes. Just take some things for yourself. And I want you to take your banjo.

"Captain Stuart says this will be a short war," Paul laughed. "Those Northern Union boys aren't ready to fight. Plus they don't know how."

"Master Paul," Thomas said. "I'd like to have supper with Martha and some of the others tonight. I need to tell them good-bye."

"Go right ahead, Thomas," said Paul. "I'll have a lot of explaining to do to my mother. And I won't need you until later."

Captain J.E.B. Stuart was everything Master Paul had said. His plumed hat sat jauntily on his head. The plume matched his scarlet cape perfectly. When the breeze lifted the cape a bit, Thomas could see a yellow sash about his waist. And the sash matched his gloves.

Captain Stuart's beautiful brown horse pawed the ground. He seemed ready to be off.

Master Paul and other young men gathered in front of Captain Stuart.

"Now, boys!" the captain shouted. "I'm glad to see you all here. Are you ready to defend our way of life?"

Cries of "Yes, sir!" filled the air.

"Are you ready to fight for the South?" the captain cried.

As the eager cries died away, Captain Stuart gave his first command to the group. "First, get fitted for uniforms. Then you'll be issued your rifle and gear.

"We'll begin our first drill in the morning," Captain Stuart continued. "Report to the drilling grounds at 8:00 sharp."

Captain Stuart saluted his new troops. And the eager young men puffed out their chests with pride as they saluted him back.

---

Paul went through two weeks of drill and practice. And finally, his chance to fight arrived.

"All assemble!" Paul and Thomas heard one morning. Paul quickly dressed and ran outside to the drilling area.

His gray jacket was belted at the waist. Gray pants, a cap, and black boots completed his uniform. The outfit made Paul look older than his 18 years.

"All fall in!" shouted the drill sergeant.

The young men rushed to their places in line.

"Captain Stuart has important news," the drill

sergeant informed the soldiers.

Captain Stuart rode briskly to the front of the young men. "We are heading into battle today," he began. "We're going to meet the enemy at Manassas by Bull Run River. We'll be riding most of the day. So I want each of you to draw three days' rations.

"It's not going to take us long to beat them Yankees!" the captain shouted.

"Attention!" shouted the drill sergeant.

The soldiers saluted as the captain turned and rode away.

Thomas quickly packed Paul's rations in a bag. Then he went to get Paul's horse. Paul would ride in formation with the others. And Thomas would ride in the wagons with the other slaves, tents, and equipment.

After two days of traveling, Paul's troop arrived at Bull Run River. They positioned themselves at Bald Hill.

The Union troops had also marched for two days. They were tired and hungry. But as they crossed a bridge into Virginia, they were confident they would beat the Southern troops.

The fighting began on Saturday morning, July 21, 1861. The two armies met at Henry House Hill.

The fighting was intense. Dust and smoke were

everywhere. As the soldiers stopped to reload, they could hardly see where to shoot.

But the shooting continued.

The Union troops seemed to forget the little training they'd had. Many men froze in place as they saw their friends and officers shot. Bodies lay where they had fallen. No one had time to tend to them or bury them.

Suddenly, the Union troops turned and ran back from where they'd come. They dropped their guns and bags in their haste.

The Union troops' fear soon turned to a panic. The roads leading back were blocked by Northern sightseers. They'd come from Washington to watch the fight.

The Union soldiers darted in and around the carriages to escape. And they realized that winning was not going to be as fast and easy as they'd thought.

The Confederates were unable to chase after the Union troops. They were tired and scared too.

The Confederate soldiers walked along the battlefield. They saw the wounded and the dead. This war would take its toll on all of them, they realized.

The unit returned to camp. The tired soldiers patted one another on the back. Everyone in the entire group felt proud.

The soldiers knew they were lucky not to have lost

any of their group. But the deaths they witnessed remained in their memories.

That night, one of the soldiers played a banjo. Everyone was in good spirits.

But the group of young men calmed as Captain Stuart rode up.

"Men," the captain said. "This was our first battle. And you did well. Since we won, I'm sure the war is almost over!"

The young men cheered and threw their caps in the air. The soldier played his banjo some more. And they all sang "Dixie."

# 9 Chapter
# Henry Goes to War

Henry and Josephine heard voices behind them. They quickly ran off the path and hid in some bushes. They watched as soldiers wearily marched north.

"They're Union soldiers," Henry said. "I wonder what's happened."

Josephine shook her head. She'd never seen so many men and in such terrible shape.

Many of the soldiers were wounded and could hardly walk. Other soldiers helped them. But the traveling was hard and slow.

"I think we should try to help them," Henry said. He pushed his way out of the bushes. He walked to the nearest man. "Can I help you?"

The wounded man was startled. "Who are you?" he asked. "What are you doing here?"

"My name's Henry," he began. "I'm a free man. And I'm trying to get back to my home in Harrisburg. Where are you coming from?"

Several of the soldiers had gathered around Henry.

"We're coming from Bull Run," one soldier said. "The rebs beat us good. We have many wounded soldiers. I guess we could use your help."

"Where's your camp?" Henry asked.

"Washington," the soldier answered. "We're the Army of the Potomac—or what's left of it. Come on. You can march along with us."

Henry motioned to Josephine. She stepped from behind the bushes.

Henry and Josephine joined the group of weary men. Henry supported a wounded soldier. And Josephine helped another by carrying his rifle and bag.

At the camp, Henry helped set up tents for the

wounded. His quick work attracted the attention of Captain Wells.

The captain introduced himself to Henry. As they shook hands, Henry told him that he was a carpenter. And he would help as long as he was needed.

"You could start building some tables," Captain Wells said. "Then the doctor can lay out his patients for surgery. I'll have some men start cutting wood right away."

"I'm traveling with a friend," Henry said. "She's already helping the men who are hurt."

"Good," said the captain. "She can find our nurses. They'll tell her what to do."

Henry knew that Josiah and Sally Turner would be worried when he didn't return. But he had a big job here. He'd try to send word to the Turners as soon as he could.

Winter was coming, and it looked as if the fighting would last for a while. So Henry helped build cabins for the officers.

General McClellan ordered the troops to drill every day. He made sure that each soldier had a place to sleep. He made sure they all helped keep the tents neat and clean.

One day, President Lincoln came with General

McClellan to inspect the troops. It was a windy day in November.

The soldiers marched proudly for two hours. They showed off their uniforms, rifles, and marching ability. President Lincoln was pleased.

It was a rainy fall. The camps were muddy. It even became hard to travel on the roads.

As Henry was roofing an officer's cabin, Captain Wells rode up. "Henry, please come down here," he said. "I need to talk to you."

"Yes, sir," replied Henry. He quickly climbed down the ladder.

"This mud is making traveling hard," said the general. "I need you to make wooden paths for us to walk on. I've assigned a group of 20 soldiers to help you. Let them know what they need to do."

"I need about one more hour to finish this roof, sir," Henry said. "And then I'll be ready."

"I'll get your men started chopping down trees," said the captain.

My men? Henry thought.

When he had finished the roof, Henry went to the soldiers who were cutting trees. He wondered if they would listen to a black man's directions.

The soldiers stopped working when they saw Henry. They gathered around to hear him.

"The logs need to be about four feet long," Henry

said. As he spoke, he showed the workers how to set each log against the other. Then they wouldn't slip or slide as people walked on them.

Henry and the soldiers worked all afternoon. At suppertime, Josephine walked by on her way to the eating tent. She grinned when she saw Henry. She stopped and waited for him.

Some of the soldiers watched. Many had noticed the way Henry and Josephine looked at each other. The soldiers grinned. Henry's got a girl, they thought.

"It's time for supper now," Henry said to the men. "Let's pick up the tools. And then we'll go eat."

When everything was picked up, Henry walked over to Josephine. "Let's go," he said.

"Have a fine evening," called one of the soldiers. Another one winked at Henry. The rest were smiling.

# Chapter 10
# MECHANICSVILLE

The Southern forces were also settling in for winter. Their tents gave little protection from the cold. So they were building log huts.

"Thomas!" Paul called one gray, cloudy morning.

"I'm here, Master Paul," Thomas replied as he entered Paul's hut.

"Thomas, I want you to build us some beds," said Paul. "It's too cold to sleep on the floor. Even with our blankets. We can put one bed against each wall. Then you can make a table and four chairs. You're really getting good with woodworking."

Thomas grinned. He enjoyed making things out of wood. He'd never done that kind of work before. And he was finding out that he had a real gift for it.

"I'm going to get you breakfast," Thomas said. "And then I'll get busy on the beds."

By noon, Thomas had built four narrow beds. He was ready to move them into the cabin.

The four soldiers let Thomas know what a great job he'd done.

"I'll start on the table after lunch," Thomas grinned.

Food was scarce that winter. The surrounding farms had been raided by the Union troops. And all the food had been taken.

So the troops ate salt pork and beef along with hardtack. They had corn bread when they could find corn.

To take the troops' minds off their hunger, Thomas often played his banjo. Their favorite songs were "Home Sweet Home," "The Girl I Left Behind Me," and "Just Before the Battle, Mother." Sometimes, the officers would join in too.

Paul was asked to go with General Stuart more now. They spied on the Army of the Potomac.

The two camps were about 30 miles from each other. Paul saw that the Union troops were building cabins and other buildings. The North didn't seem to be readying for battle.

General Robert E. Lee, the commander of the Army of Northern Virginia, and his able officer, General Stonewall Jackson, were very interested in the latest report.

"We'll let them make the first move," General Jackson said. "We need the time to gather supplies for the men."

General Lee agreed. He saw that many soldiers were shoeless, and their clothing was in tatters.

Still, General Lee was worried. The Union troops were getting closer and closer to Richmond. And that was the Confederate capital.

So General Stuart and his troops circled the Union camps. They looked for weak spots where attacks could take place.

Paul enjoyed the spying missions. There was little danger of fighting. He didn't have to see anyone die.

General Stuart reported to General Lee after his latest spying mission. "Sir, there are several weak spots. Two of my men have reports for you."

General Lee stepped outside his office. Paul and

another soldier quickly saluted.

"What did you see?" General Lee asked.

"The Union troops are spread out very thin at Mechanicsville," Paul began. "Especially on the sides. Most of the troops are gathered in the middle."

"Good job, soldiers," said General Lee.

Then the two generals stepped back inside the office. They were ready to plan their first attack.

---

The next battle was at Mechanicsville—just northeast of Richmond. General Jackson and his Confederate troops were late in arriving. So the Union troops were able to defeat the small group of Confederates that were there.

As darkness fell, Captain Wells found Henry. "I need you to go back to the battlefield, Henry," he said. "To search for wounded. Take some men with you. And take two or three of the wagons."

"Yes, sir," replied Henry. "Right away, sir."

Henry wasn't looking forward to this job. He said good-bye to Josephine. Then he gathered five men and went back to the battleground.

It was a dark, cloudy night. The men's small lanterns didn't give much light.

The men wrapped cloths over their noses and mouths. The smell of death was very strong. Then they began their search.

Many of their soldiers were found and carried to the wagons. Rifles, bags, and canteens were also picked up. The troops would be able to use them.

From not far away, the sound of music and singing could be heard. Henry and the other soldiers were curious. So they crept to where the sound was coming from.

Henry saw soldiers singing around a campfire. One was playing the banjo. As Henry got closer, he couldn't believe his eyes! There were black men singing too. And one of them looked a lot like him! Could it be . . . ?

Henry wanted to move closer, but he knew he'd be seen. And probably shot.

Just then, the music stopped. The men said good night. They walked away from the fire into the darkness.

Henry decided he'd come back the next night. If the man he saw was Thomas, Henry knew he'd find a way for them to be together.

But the next day, Henry was kept busy. All day he helped troops cross the swollen Chickahominy River. The next few days were the same.

Later in the week, Henry was helping with the wounded. Spies reported that the Confederates were drawing closer. The Union troops retreated.

During the next two days, General McClellan arrived with fresh troops. But they were not very successful.

The Confederates were also having problems. General Jackson's troops arrived late again. The Confederates missed their chance to attack the Union's supply train. It left Richmond safely.

Over 16,000 Union soldiers and 20,000 Confederate soldiers were dead or wounded after seven days of battles. The Union and Confederate troops had to rest up and restock their supplies.

Henry wanted to sneak over to the Confederate camp again. To see if that man was his brother. But there were too many miles between them now. Henry was frustrated and forced to wait again.

Chapter 11

# MEETING AND PARTING

A few days later, General Stuart asked to see Paul.

"Paul, I need you for a special job," the general said. "General Lee's wife needs an escort from her home to Richmond. She wants to be with her husband."

"Yes, sir," said Paul. "I'll be glad to help."

"You'll leave tomorrow," said the general. "I'll send a letter explaining your trip in case anyone should ask."

Paul rushed off to tell Thomas about the assignment. They'd both be leaving the next morning.

---

The trip from Arlington to Richmond was quiet. The general's wife didn't complain, even though it was a bumpy trip.

As they neared town, another wagon was coming toward them from the opposite direction. The road was narrow. So Thomas guided the horses over to the side to wait for the wagon to pass.

As the wagon neared, Thomas's eyes widened. He couldn't believe what he was seeing! It was like looking in a mirror. Could it be? After all these years?

The driver of the wagon stared back at Thomas. His mouth hung open.

The two men studied each other. Then they both broke into wide grins.

"Whoa!" Henry called to the horses. By this time, Thomas was running toward him.

"Henry?" asked Thomas. He held up his hand.

Henry held up his hand too. They had the same crooked little fingers!

"Thomas!" called Henry. He jumped down from

his wagon.

"I always knew I'd find you," said Henry as they hugged each other.

By this time, a crowd had gathered around them. They looked in wonder at the two men who looked exactly alike. The happiness spread. And soon, everyone was laughing.

About that time, two Union officers rode up.

"What's going on?" demanded one of the officers. He jumped down from his horse.

Paul took out the letter. He handed it to the officer.

After the letter had been read, the Union officers ordered everyone to move along.

Henry and Thomas knew they had to obey. As Thomas returned to his horse, he shouted, "I'll find you again, Henry! And then we'll never be apart!"

Thomas rode alongside Paul. "Do you remember the story about me having a twin? And my father taking him and escaping?"

"I remember," Paul nodded.

"We looked at each other," Thomas continued. "And we knew. It was like looking in a mirror. And our crooked little fingers were the same!"

"What was your brother doing in Richmond?" Paul asked. "And did you ask about your father?"

"I didn't have time to ask him anything," Thomas replied. "It all happened so quickly."

"He's on the other side, Thomas," said Paul. "It's going to be hard to find him. But I know how much this means to you. I'll try to help you."

When Henry returned to camp, he found Josephine. He told her all about Thomas and how they'd met.

"I know you and Thomas will be together soon, Henry," Josephine said. She gently squeezed Henry's hand.

Henry was speechless as she held his hand. He just nodded at Josephine. He believed every word she said.

Several weeks later, Paul went along on another spying mission. They found the main storage location of the Union army supplies near a railroad junction.

General Lee sent Jackson and his troops to take this supply depot. They were able to capture it with little effort. There weren't many soldiers guarding it.

Then the real fighting began. After three days, the Union was defeated in the second battle of Bull Run. The Union army retreated to Washington. The rain was so heavy that day, the Confederates were unable to follow them.

That night, there was no singing or banjo playing. The heavy rain kept the Confederates inside their cabins and tents.

# Chapter 12
# Thomas Abandoned

One evening, Captain Wells found Henry building more tables. The captain asked Henry to lead a group of men to search the battlefields.

"I know the battle is still going on," said Captain Wells. "But see if you can find wounded men. We may be able to save their lives if we get to them right away."

Henry quickly picked up his tools. He gathered a few other men who were working around camp. And they headed toward a wagon.

I'm never going to get used to this chore, thought Henry.

"We'll go around to the right side," Henry said to the other men. "That's where most of the fighting was today. And hopefully, the fighting has moved on."

As Henry and the other men came up over a small rise, they gasped. Below them were bodies as far as they could see.

Henry helped direct the horses and wagon down the hill. He could see a creek at the bottom.

As the men traveled down the hill, they looked for the wounded. They also collected rifles, shoes, canteens, and other gear for their troops.

There were so many bodies. Henry was afraid they'd never find the men who were still alive.

"Can anybody hear me?" shouted Henry. "We're here to help!"

Henry heard a weak groan to his left. So he and another man hurried over. They found two men who were barely alive. Henry and the other man carried them to the wagon.

Then the searchers found two more wounded men.

It was quickly turning dark now. The searchers had done all they could. So they started back up the hill to camp.

"Who won today?" Henry asked another searcher.

"I don't think anybody won, Henry," the man said. "Only death. Death was the winner for sure."

Henry was glad that the troops were moving north for supplies. He'd seen enough death for a while.

---

Thomas searched the faces of the soldiers returning from battle. The sunlight was fading, so he lit a lantern.

Thomas still hadn't seen Paul. He walked around camp. He looked for Paul's horse.

Thomas looked for one of Paul's friends. Finally, he saw one. The man was sitting by the fire. His eyes seemed glazed over. And he hadn't touched his meal.

"Excuse me, sir," said Thomas. "Have you seen Paul Walker?"

The man wiped his mouth on his dirty sleeve. "Paul?" he said. "He's not the only one I haven't seen. There's been so much killing. And so many bodies . . ." The man's voice died away.

"Thank you, sir," Thomas said as he backed away.

Was Paul dead? he wondered. There was only one way to find out.

Before dawn, Thomas got up. He hitched a horse to one of the wagons. Then, as quietly as possible, he headed back in the direction of the fighting.

As the sun rose, Thomas could see bodies everywhere. How would he find Paul?

The odor of death was everywhere. Thomas tied his bandanna over his nose and mouth. Then he tied the horse to a stump and began his search.

The only sounds Thomas heard were flies buzzing and birds chirping.

As the sun rose higher, Thomas was able to see the men more clearly. Thomas searched until the sun was overhead.

Then Thomas saw him. He sat down next to Paul and cried. What was he to do now?

Finally, Thomas knew he had to move on. So he pulled Paul out from the other bodies. Then he carried Paul's body and gear to the wagon.

Thomas headed back. As he neared the camp, he realized there were no noises. And as he rounded a thick clump of bushes, he saw that the troops had moved.

Thirsty and hungry, Thomas knew what he had to do. First he had to bury Paul.

Thomas searched the abandoned camp for a shovel. He found a canteen and took a deep drink. As he drank, he spotted a branch lying on the ground next to a nearby bush.

The ground around the bush was soft. So Thomas began digging. After a while, he had dug a hole large enough for Paul's body.

Thomas was hot and tired. And his arms and legs ached. But he worked to finish the job.

Thomas carried Paul to the grave. He laid him down as gently as possible. Then he covered him with the soft dirt. Then he prayed for Paul's soul.

Thomas went back to the wagon. He didn't know where to go or what to do. For the first time in his life, there was no one around to give him orders.

Thomas searched the dead men's bags for food. He found enough to keep his stomach from hurting.

Then he gathered wood and built a fire. He knew he had to keep warm through the night.

Once the fire was going, Thomas took care of the horse. He unhitched the wagon and led the horse to a grassy area. Then Thomas settled next to the fire for the night.

The next morning, Thomas was awakened by the neighing of the horse. The sun was just beginning to rise. Thomas shivered in the early morning air.

Thomas remembered the terrible events of the day before. He had never felt so alone.

He led the horse to the nearby creek. He made sure to stay away from the bodies on the hill.

As Thomas and the horse took a drink of the cool creek water, Thomas spied some fish. They were lazily swimming against the current. He had an idea.

He ran back up the hill to the wagon. He emptied one of the men's bags. Then he returned to the creek with the bag.

He held the bag under water and stayed very still. As the fish swam near, he scooped the bag through the water. Nothing!

Thomas was too hungry to give up. And finally, he caught a fish! After a while, he had three fish on the bank of the creek.

Thomas put the fish in the bag and led the horse back to the wagon. He gathered wood again and lit the fire. Soon the smell of the cooking fish was everywhere.

As he ate, Thomas made a decision. He knew he should return to the plantation and tell Master Walker about Paul's death. But his longing for freedom was strong. And his longing to see his twin brother was even stronger!

So after hitching the horse to the wagon, Thomas

climbed aboard. As the warm sun shone on his face, he smiled. He would follow the Union troops. Then he knew he'd find Henry.

# Chapter 13
# FINDING HENRY

Two uneventful days later, Thomas rode into a Union camp. There were many soldiers working. Thomas thought that they were gathering supplies. And since they were Union soldiers, Thomas didn't expect any trouble.

"What are you doing here?" said a loud voice behind Thomas.

Thomas looked around as a Union captain rode up alongside of him. His heart leaped into his throat. He was afraid he'd be caught as a runaway slave.

"Henry," the captain began. "I thought you were working on the bridge."

"Excuse me, sir," said a very relieved Thomas. "My name is Thomas. Henry is my twin brother. Is he nearby?"

"I guess you are twins!" chuckled the captain. "So Thomas is your name?"

Thomas nodded. "Yes, sir."

"Henry is working nearby," said the captain. "My name is Captain Wells. I'll take you where your brother was working earlier. Follow me."

As they neared the Rappahannock River, Thomas could see many men working.

"What are the men doing, sir?" Thomas asked.

"General Burnside wants to move troops to Fredericksburg," said the captain. "The river is swollen because of all the rain. So Henry and the others are building bridges across the river."

"I'll bet they could use my help," Thomas said.

"I'm sure they can," said the captain.

Thomas climbed down from the wagon to search for Henry. And finally, he spotted him.

"Henry!" Thomas called as he ran toward his brother. "Henry!"

Henry heard his name being called. He looked up and couldn't believe his eyes! He dropped his saw and ran too.

As Henry and Thomas met, they threw their arms around each other. Then they grinned and began talking at the same time. The men who were helping with the bridge smiled as they gathered around the two brothers.

"Why, Henry's got a twin," one soldier said.

"We're glad you've found each other, Thomas and Henry," said Captain Wells. "After work tonight, we'll have a celebration!"

"Yes, sir!" said Henry.

"Thomas, why don't you come with me now," said the captain. "You've traveled far and must need some rest and something to eat."

"No, sir," said Thomas. "I've found my brother. And I'm not leaving him. I'm here to help."

After the captain left, Henry showed Thomas what to do. The brothers worked side by side, lashing the pontoons together.

"General Burnside wants to cross the river. But it's too high," explained Henry. "The Confederates are holed up downriver on the other side. In Fredericksburg."

The two brothers didn't have much time for talk. But there was one question that couldn't wait.

"What about our dad?" Thomas asked. "Where is he? And why didn't he ever come for me?"

Henry told him of Byron's death. He assured Thomas that he'd explain everything later.

---

That evening the brothers and Josephine ate together. It was hard knowing where to begin. But both young men managed to tell each other about the past 18 years.

Josephine listened to how much Thomas and Henry had been through. She thought about how long they'd both had to wait for this moment.

"I've got a family now," Henry said proudly. He looked at Thomas and Josephine. "And when this war's over, we'll settle down together."

Late into the night the brothers talked. And for several nights after that, they found more and more stories to share.

They weren't getting much sleep. But they didn't care.

Thomas and Henry worked together for several weeks. Josephine continued to help the sick and wounded soldiers.

Finally, the five pontoon bridges were in place.

And on a chilly December day, the Union army crossed the river. They got ready for battle.

The Union troops attacked the next day. Thomas, Henry, and Josephine stayed behind. They knew their jobs would come soon enough.

"Our next job will be to search for wounded, Thomas," Henry explained.

"I've done a lot of that already," Thomas said sadly.

As the end of the day neared, Thomas and Henry took a wagon across the river. They knew it was dangerous for them. But they had to get the wounded men back across the river to save them.

The brothers worked for three days. They'd cross the river and gather the wounded. Then they'd take them back to camp.

Josephine was always waiting for them. She worried. She knew what they were doing was dangerous.

On the third day, Thomas and Henry crossed the bridge to gather the wounded. But this time, they met Union soldiers in a retreat. The brothers knew their trip would be risky. But they were determined to continue.

There were fewer and fewer gunshots now. Henry guessed that the Confederates had many wounded too. Henry and Thomas took the stretcher and began searching.

"Look for movement, Thomas," said Henry. "And

keep down low."

Thomas and Henry had found four wounded Union soldiers. The two brothers climbed on the wagon to head back.

"Let's go," Henry said.

But before Henry could say more, a bullet struck him in the throat. He grabbed his neck. Blood sprayed between his fingers. He slowly sank to the wagon seat.

Thomas held Henry to keep him from falling from the wagon.

I can't lose him now, Thomas thought desperately.

Thomas drove as quickly as he could back across the river. He began yelling to Josephine as soon as he thought she could hear him.

Thomas skidded to a stop in front of the medical tents. Josephine was waiting.

Many hands helped unload the wounded soldiers. But Thomas would let no one touch Henry. Thomas carried Henry into a tent. And gently, he laid Henry down. Josephine worked frantically to stop the bleeding.

"This bullet has got to come out," said the doctor.

Those were the last words Thomas heard. He passed out and fell to the ground.

"Take him outside," the doctor said. "He's probably never seen so much blood."

Josephine and another nurse dragged Thomas

outside the tent. They propped him up against a tree. Then Josephine returned to help with Henry.

Outside, the cold air woke Thomas. He sat up and a soldier offered him a drink of water.

"Here, have a drink," the soldier said. "They're doing everything they can for your brother."

Thomas managed to drink a little water. Then he stood up.

"I've got to go help Henry now," Thomas said. He thanked the soldier and went back inside the tent.

The doctor had already removed the bullet. And he was now stitching up the wound the bullet had made.

"He's lost a lot of blood," the doctor said. "If he can make it through the night, his chances are good."

When the doctor finished, Henry was moved to another tent. Thomas and Josephine stayed by his side all night. To help pass the time, Thomas visited with a soldier in a nearby bed.

The soldier told Thomas about all the things Henry had helped with—the furniture, the cabins, and the bridge.

The next morning, a doctor walked into the tent to check on the patients. He finally got to Henry's bed.

"How's he doing?" Josephine asked.

After examining Henry, the doctor spoke up. "He should make it, but he'll need plenty of rest. And there's always the risk of infection.

"The bullet has done a lot of damage," the doctor continued. "He may not be able to talk."

Thomas knew that not being able to speak would be hard for Henry. But he just wanted him to live.

"The doctors are always busy working on the soldiers," said Josephine. "They may not be able to give Henry the care he needs." After much thought, Thomas made a decision.

"The closest place to get help is the Walker plantation," said Thomas. "Martha will make Henry better."

Thomas knew he could be walking into trouble by returning to the plantation. But he knew that Henry needed help. And he knew he had to tell Master Walker about Paul's death.

The trip would be hard for Henry. But Thomas thought Henry would get better care from Martha.

So Thomas and Josephine hitched Henry's wagon to his horse. With Henry fading in and out of consciousness, they set out.

Henry groaned as he bumped around in the wagon. But Josephine stayed by his side. She dripped water through his lips and washed his face. She tried to help cool his body.

Traveling was slow. Thomas tried to stay away from the main roads. That way, they wouldn't run into any Confederate troops. Still he didn't want to bump

Henry around any more than he had to.

Finally after a day and a half, Henry, Thomas, and Josephine arrived at the Walker plantation.

The first person they saw was William, the overseer. He just stared at the three in the wagon as they passed. Thomas drove straight to Martha's cabin. And he and Josephine settled Henry into Martha's bed.

While Josephine watched over Henry, Thomas went to find Master Walker. But the master was already on his way. William was with him.

*William must've told him,* thought Thomas.

Thomas took a deep breath. He would tell the master everything—beginning with Paul's death.

# Chapter 14
# FULL CIRCLE

Master Walker was very saddened by the news about Paul. After hearing the details of Paul's heroic actions and his death, Master Walker turned to walk away. His shoulders were slumped.

"Excuse me, sir," said Thomas.

Master Walker stopped and turned around. He waited for Thomas to continue.

"My brother, Henry, is here. And he's hurt badly," Thomas said. "He needs help."

Thomas was afraid of what the master might do to his brother. After all, he was a runaway slave. But right now, Thomas was more worried about his brother's life.

"Martha can help him," said Thomas. "Can I go get her?"

"No," said Master Walker. "No, you stay with your brother. William can get her."

Then the master turned again. He walked toward the Big House. He had to tell his wife about their only son's death.

Thomas could tell that William wasn't happy. But the master had given an order. And William had to obey. He got on his horse and rode off.

A relieved Thomas went into Martha's cabin to check on Henry. Josephine was still holding a wet rag to his forehead.

"Martha will be here soon," said Thomas. And he held Henry's hand in his, willing him to get better.

---

When Henry awoke, he felt a great pain in his neck. He opened his eyes. A strange woman was bending over him. She was putting something on his neck. Henry tried to wipe it away but was too weak.

"Henry," the woman said. "Be still now. I'm trying to make you feel better."

Henry looked closer. The woman knew him. But he had no idea who she was.

"Oh, Henry," said the woman. "I thought I'd never see you or your brother again. I'm Martha. I raised your daddy."

Henry knew who she was now. His father had talked of Martha. And Henry knew that meant he was back on the plantation.

Thomas walked into the cabin then. He was relieved to see Henry awake. He called to Josephine. Henry's eyes lit up when he saw her.

Josephine sat next to Henry and held his hand. "You're going to get better now," she said. "Martha and I will take care of you."

Henry fell asleep with a smile on his face.

The next day, Henry was able to drink some broth. It hurt going down, but he was hungry. That was a good sign.

Thomas was still worried about what Master Walker would do. But he knew he must talk to him soon. So he walked toward the Big House.

Thomas walked into the cookhouse first. Nancy

was preparing dinner. She ran to give him a big hug. There were tears in her eyes.

"Oh, Thomas!" she cried. "We were so worried about you. We're glad you're back safely! And Henry too.

"Oh, how we'll miss Master Paul," she continued. "He was so young."

After a short conversation, Thomas told her he'd come to see Master Walker. He told Nancy good-bye and went to the back door of the Big House.

Thomas knocked on the door. The door was opened quickly. When Thomas asked to speak to the master, the house servant left to announce Thomas's arrival.

After a few minutes, Thomas was led into the house. The house servant took him to the master's library.

"Come in, Thomas," said Master Walker. "I figured you'd come to see me."

"Yes, sir," said Thomas. "I'm sure sorry I had to come back with such bad news."

"Yes, Paul's mother is taking it very badly," said the master. "And I guess I am too."

"I was wondering what's to become of my brother, Henry," said Thomas. "He's too sick to be punished for running away. I'd like you to punish me instead."

Master Walker looked at him in surprise. "No one's

going to get punished," he said. "Henry was just a baby when his father took him."

Relief washed over Thomas. He thanked the master for his kindness.

"My son was everything to me," said Master Walker. "And now he's dead. I don't have anyone left to help me with this plantation.

"And my heart is just not into running it myself," continued the master. "Paul died trying to protect a dying way of life. And I don't know what I'm going to do without him."

"I'm sorry, sir," said Thomas. "I wish there was something I could do."

"There is," said Master Walker. "Gather everyone at Martha's cabin after supper. I have some things to say."

"Yes, sir," said Thomas. As he left, he wondered what the master would say to them.

---

Master Walker approached the group of slaves. They quieted, curious about why the master had gathered them.

"I have no one left to help me run the plantation now that Paul's gone," the master began. "I'm getting too old to run it myself. Mrs. Walker and I have decided to move to town.

"I'm going to keep this land, though," he continued. "You can stay here and farm it if you wish. Otherwise, you are free to leave. I will have the necessary papers for you tomorrow."

Then the master turned and walked away.

The stunned group of people just looked at one another. And finally, they began to sing. They sang songs about the promised land. That's where many of them wanted to go—to the North.

Josephine, Thomas, and Martha went into Martha's cabin. They told Henry the good news.

"As soon as you can travel, we'll go north," said Thomas. "I know you had a good life in Harrisburg. And we'll go back with you. We're a family now. You, me, Josephine, and Martha. And nothing and no one will separate us again!"